For those in my life to whom, upon parting,
it felt too soon to say goodbye

G. P. PUTNAM'S SONS
An imprint of Penguin Random House LLC, New York

Visit us online at penguinrandomhouse.com

Library of Congress Cataloging-in-Publication Data
Names: Marcero, Deborah, author, illustrator.
Title: In a jar / Deborah Marcero.
Description: New York: G. P. Putnam's Sons, [2020]
Summary: When Llewellyn, a little rabbit who collects ordinary things in jars,
meets a young girl named Evelyn, he joins with her to capture the extraordinary.
Identifiers: LCCN 2018056322 | ISBN 9780525514596 (hardcover) |
ISBN 9780525514602 (epub fxl cpb) | ISBN 9780525514626 (kf8/kindle)
Subjects: | CYAC: Collectors and collecting—Fiction. | Friendship—Fiction. | Rabbits—Fiction.
Classification: LCC PZ7.1.M3699 In 2020 | DDC [E]—dc23
LC record available at https://lccn.loc.gov/2018056322
Manufactured in China by RR Donnelley Asia Printing Solutions Ltd.
ISBN 9780525514596
10   9   8   7   6   5   4

Design by Eileen Savage | Text set in Tuff Normal
The art was done in pencil, watercolor, ink, and digital media.

IN A JAR

DEBORAH MARCERO

putnam

G. P. PUTNAM'S SONS

Llewellyn was a collector.
He collected things in jars.

When he held a jar and peered inside,
Llewellyn remembered all the wonderful
things he had seen and done.

He collected small, ordinary things,

like buttercups,

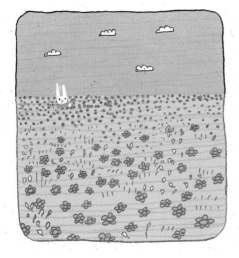  

feathers,

and heart-shaped stones.

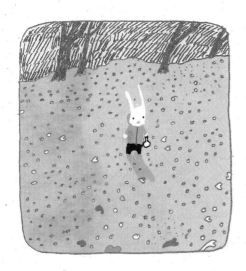  

One night, the sunset painted the sky the color of
tart cherry syrup. Llewellyn ventured down to the
shore with as many jars as he could carry.

A little girl named Evelyn was there too.

Llewellyn scooped that cherry light into his jars.

And when he was done, he gave one to Evelyn.

Evelyn took the jar home.

And to her surprise, it glowed through the night
with the memory of that sunset.

From then on, Llewellyn and Evelyn collected things together.
They collected things hard to hold, like rainbows,

the sound of the ocean,

 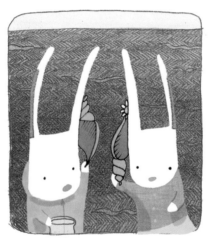 

and the wind just before snow falls.

They collected things you might not think would
even fit in a jar. But somehow, they did.

They collected the wonders of winter . . .

the newness of spring . . .

and the long days and shadows of summer.

Over time, their jars
filled the walls of
Llewellyn's house.

But one day, Evelyn had sad news.

Her family was moving to a new town.

Too soon, it was time
to say goodbye.

With Evelyn gone,
Llewellyn's heart felt like an empty jar.

One night, Llewellyn lay awake. Falling stars
glittered against the dark sky. He wondered
if Evelyn could see them too.

That gave him an idea.

Llewellyn tiptoed out into the moonless night
and collected the meteor shower in a jar.

The next day, he prepared a package.

When the box arrived and Evelyn opened the jar,
the stars in the night sky fell around her.

Evelyn knew just what to do.
She collected the sounds,

the crowds,

  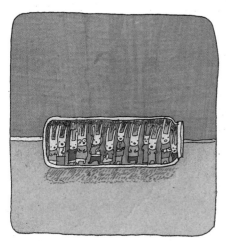

and the bright night lights of her new home

and sent them all to Llewellyn.

And so, when the golden leaves of autumn began to fall once again, Llewellyn set out to collect a jarful for Evelyn.

A little boy named Max was there too.

Luckily, Llewellyn had brought an extra jar.